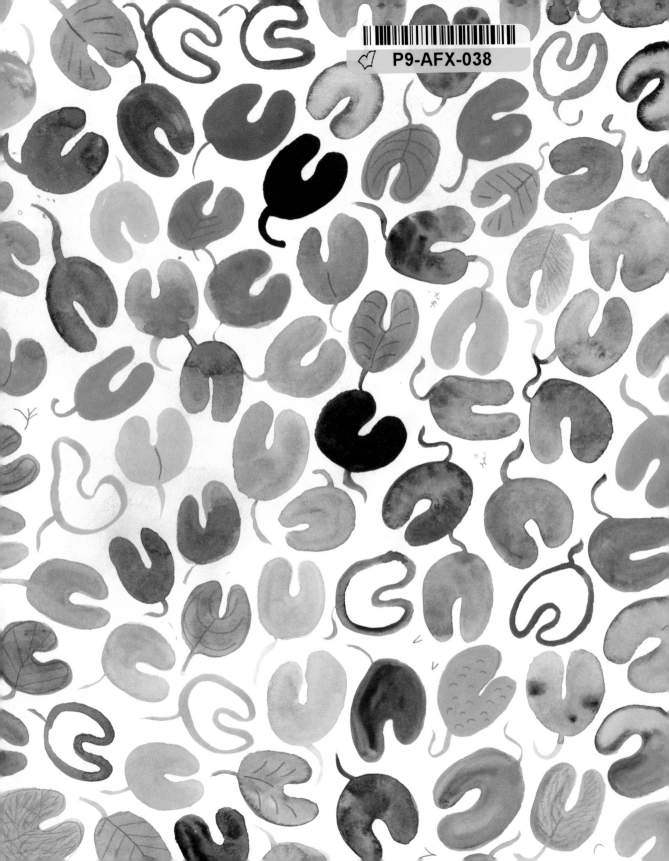

www.enchahntedlion.com

First English-language edition published in 2018 by Enchanted Lion Books
67 West Street, 317A, Brooklyn, NY 11222
Text and illustrations Copyright © 2016 by Lilla Piratförlaget AB
First published in Swedish as *Utflyktarna*
All rights reserved under International
and Pan-American Copyright Conventions
A CIP record is on file with the Library of Congress.

ISBN 978-1-59270-245-9

Printed in China by RR Donnelley Asia Printing Solutions Ltd.

1 3 5 7 9 10 8 6 4 2

Emma AdBåge

THE GRAND EXPEDITION

TRANSLATED FROM SWEDISH BY ANNIE PRIME

ENCHANTED LION BOOKS

NEW YORK

Iben and I have made a decision.

We are going on an expedition.
Our own expedition,
just the two of us.
With treats and blankets and
a cozy tent to sleep in.

We find a good bag and pack everything we need.
A pocket flashlight, a nature book, a toy knife
for each of us, and something to snuggle with.
Iben takes a jump rope, too.

"In case we need a lasso!"

Now we just need treats.

But all the treats are finished. The cupboards are empty.
We search high and low.

"Take those pickles then," Dad says.

"WHAT?" we say, even though we hear what he says.
"We need treats!"

But there are no treats. And Dad says he can't
conjure them out of thin air.

"BOO!" we say and sulk for a long time.

Then we leave.

We know exactly where we are going,
because we have already put up the tent.
It is next to a great big rock. Perfect.
Now we can stay out all day.

We make our beds and set out
our things. Then we sit around.
I flip through the nature book
and find a squashed ant
between the pages.

"Cool!" says Iben.

I save the ant. Soon it gets dark.

Time to sleep at last! We nibble on the pickles
and sing some nursery rhymes.
Iben turns the flashlight on. It feels cozy.

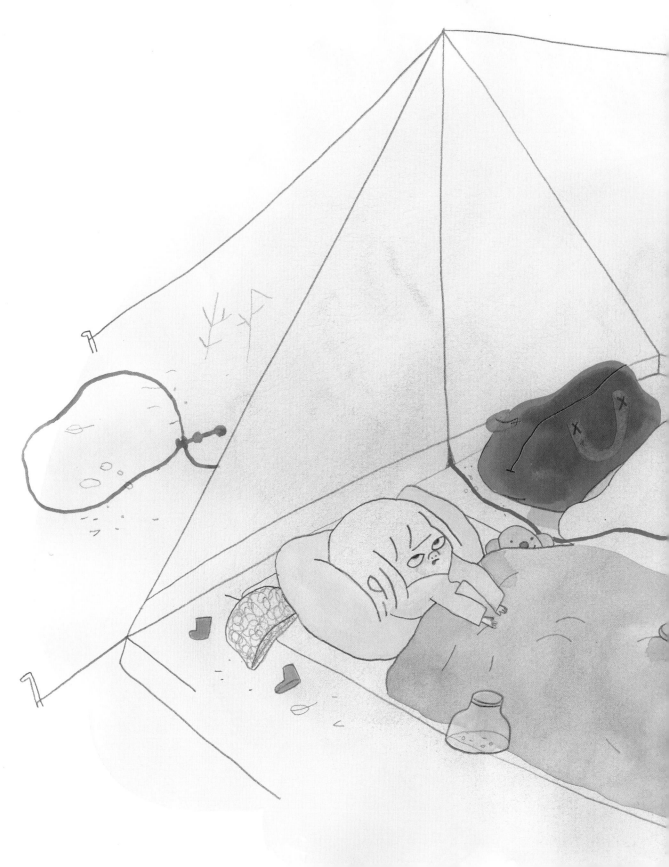

Then we run out of pickles and nursery rhymes.
We are sooo bored!

"I think I need to poop," I say.

And Iben feels something sharp,
right between the shoulder blades.
Then we hear a mosquito. It's no good anymore.

Dad looks surprised when we come home,
but we act the same as usual.

Iben falls asleep immediately.
I go to the bathroom to poop.
Then I watch TV with Dad for a bit.
A movie about crocodiles with fast music.
Dad gets out some cheese puffs.

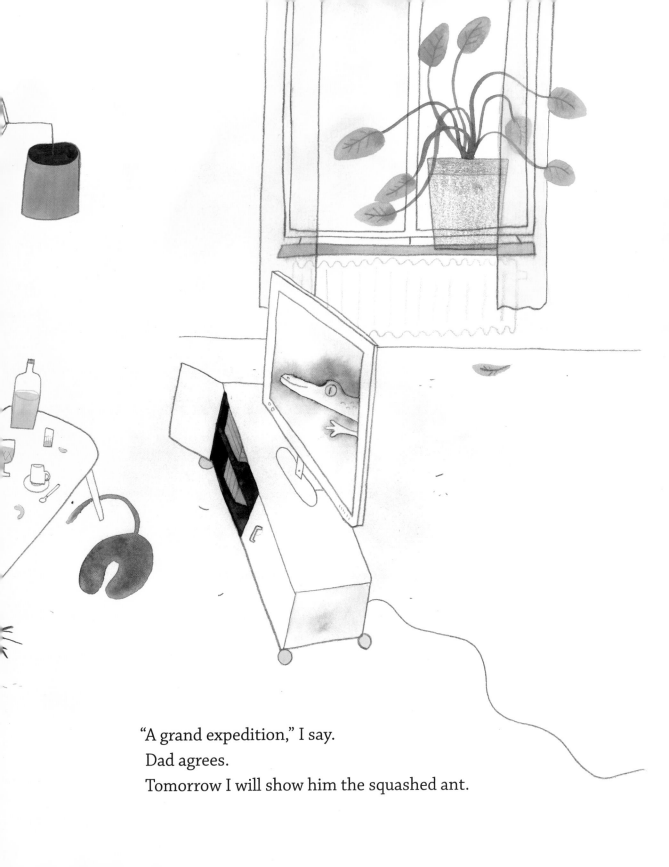

"A grand expedition," I say.
Dad agrees.
Tomorrow I will show him the squashed ant.

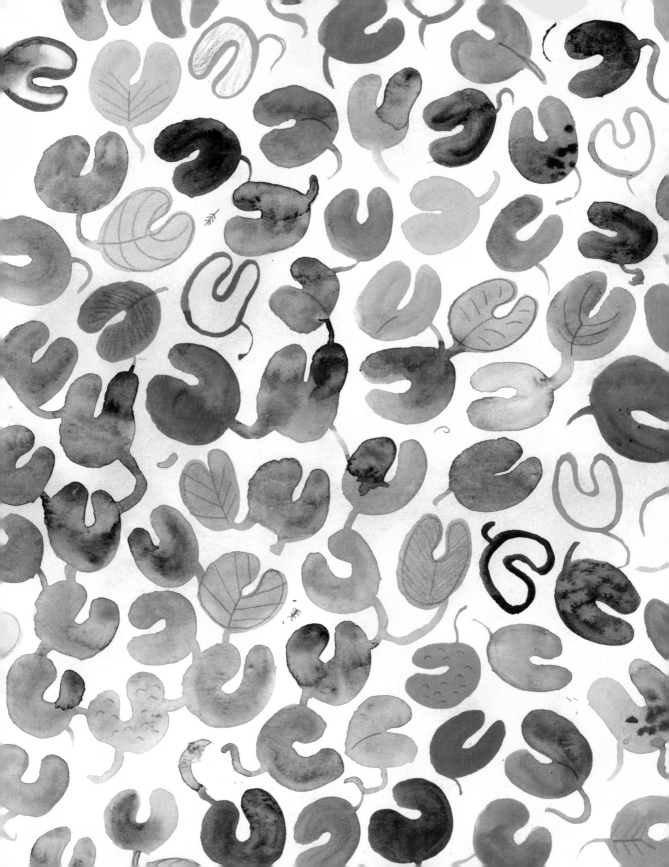